For Alexandra
D.M.

For Jess,
with lots of love
D.G.

Text copyright © 1993 by David Martin
Illustrations copyright © 1993 by Debi Gliori

First U.S. edition 1993

Library of Congress Cataloging-in-Publication Data
Martin, David, 1944–
Lizzie and her kitty / written by David Martin ; illustrated by Debi Gliori. —
1st U.S. ed.
Summary: Lizzie cuddles with her kitty and ends up with pudding in her hair.
ISBN 1-56402-058-4
[1. Cats—Fiction.   2. Stories in rhyme.]
I. Gliori, Debi, ill. II. Title.
PZ8.3.M4115Lir   1993
[E]—dc20   92-54405

10 9 8 7 6 5 4 3 2 1

Printed in Italy

The pictures for this book
were done in watercolor.

Candlewick Press
2067 Massachusetts Avenue
Cambridge, Massachusetts 02140

Lizzie
and Her Kitty

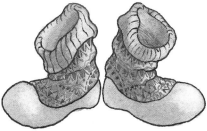

DAVID MARTIN

illustrated by
DEBI GLIORI

CANDLEWICK PRESS
CAMBRIDGE, MASSACHUSETTS

Where is Lizzie?
Lizzie's in her chair.

Where is Lizzie's pudding?
Dripping from her hair.

Where is Lizzie's kitty?
Kitty's on the floor.

Kitty's licking pudding
And hoping for some more.

Now where is Lizzie?
Lizzie's at the sink.

She's turning on the water
So she can get a drink.

Now where is kitty?
With Lizzie in her chair.

And what is kitty doing?
Licking Lizzie's hair.

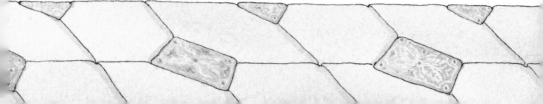